I0583489

We all carry hidden wounds—silent pains that eat away at our spirit and leave us feeling alone. Sharing these buried struggles is difficult; others might see them as odd, which only heightens our sense of isolation.

Healing from such emotional weight can feel impossible. We turn to passing escapes like wine or opioids, hoping for a moment of relief. Yet these only deepen our suffering. Is there anyone capable of untangling our private sorrows, those quiet cries echoing in the murky space between wakefulness and sleep?

One event in particular is etched into my heart—a memory that refuses to fade. It's beyond most people's understanding and casts a dark shadow over my life. As a novelist, I've lived through experiences that still haunt my soul.

I don't write to change minds or seek validation. My real fear is leaving this world without deciphering the mysteries locked within me. In a world that often misunderstands me, I find comfort in silence.

Through writing, I follow my own shadow, allowing myself to explore the depths of my soul. My words draw me closer to my true self, freeing me from the burdens of the world.

Yet doubts remain. Are the people around me sincere, or do wolves in sheep's clothing test my resolve? Are my emotions merely illusions, severed from any real foundation? These questions swirl within me, compelling me to seek clarity and confront the shadows that blur my existence.

By laying my thoughts on paper, I hope to connect with my most hidden inner realms. I aim to uncover the truth about the world I inhabit. Has even a single ray of sunlight ever pierced my gloom? No—it was nothing more than a fleeting, otherworldly flash of relentless sorrow, brief triumph, fading beauty, and enduring pain. It vanished like smoke, leaving me longing for a peace and understanding that forever seem just out of reach.

It's been two months and four days since she left this world, yet her glowing eyes, lit by wonder, remain vivid in my mind. I dare not utter her name, for she was a being of delicate grace. Her gaze, once vibrant with curiosity, now resides beyond the cruelty of our mortal plane. I won't burden her memory with life's harshness.

Our final moments are scorched into my soul like a perpetual flame. Her gentle eyes met mine, conveying a depth no words could hold. In that silent exchange, we shared the promise of lifetimes past and future. Even as her body weakened, her spirit wrapped itself around me once more, a whispered vow in the emptiness that we would meet again.

Her absence tore open a well of grief. I sealed myself off from the world, unable to face either innocence or guilt. Wine and opium became my desperate attempt to numb the ache of her memory. Time lost all shape as I drowned in the crushing stillness of longing.

In the midst of my sorrow, I discovered a surprising refuge: decorating pen case covers with elaborate designs. This spellbinding pastime, combined with the numbing haze of wine and opium, granted me a brief escape from time's unyielding march.

My home stood alone on the city's outskirts, a forgotten edifice removed from any sense of life. It loomed over a cluster of modest mud houses, as if they pressed together for warmth against the endless void. I often cursed the tasteless architect behind this strange, discordant structure.

When I closed my eyes, bright images of my meticulously designed pen cases crowded my thoughts. They weren't ordinary pen cases—they were masterworks, lingering reminders of a time when beauty truly mattered.

The cheerless, stifling house I lived in felt like the polar opposite of those memories. Its looming form weighed on my spirit, overshadowing the quiet surroundings. Then I saw her. Her piercing eyes forced me to question all I knew about myself and my art.

Still, despite my uncertainty, my love for creation endured. It felt as though some invisible force guided my hands while I brought my visions to life. Scene after scene poured onto the page, each centered on a single cypress tree.

An elderly man, monk-like in appearance, sat deep in thought beneath the tree. Opposite him, a young woman in a black dress offered a blue lotus flower. Were these visions from my past, or dreams lodged in my mind? I couldn't say, but I was driven to capture them.

My art took on a life of its own, sweeping me away to the bustling streets of India, where my uncle sold my pen cases and sent the funds back home. Those sales allowed me to keep creating, determined to preserve the fleeting images that haunted me.

I was fueled by an intense need to cling to these memories, however insubstantial they might be. My art became my link to the past, my means of giving the ephemeral a lasting form. And so I continued, channeling my entire being into each piece, letting my pen cases and sketches tell the story of a beauty I refused to lose.

Life had worn me down, carving deep scars into my soul. The weight of my private struggles pulled me away from the colorful world of art I'd once loved. I could barely stand the thought of painting another pen case.

Two months and four days ago, on Sizdah Bedar, when city dwellers retreated to the countryside, I remained in my room, absorbed in the gentle rhythm of painting. As evening arrived, the door creaked open—and there stood my long-lost uncle, the family's roving adventurer.

He was a bit stooped, as though the years had pressed down on him. A bright, travel-worn shawl wrapped around his head, and his faded cloak hinted at a life of secrets. His lively eyes gleamed despite the wrinkles surrounding them, and his weathered lips spoke of days spent beneath wide-open skies. When he entered, the air carried the smells of the ocean, sweat, and something tangy. The raw freedom in his appearance fascinated me. He looked like the father I had never truly known, possessing a charm that time hadn't dulled.

I felt an immediate pull toward him, an overwhelming need to feel the roughness of his hands—hands that, in my mind, should have been my father's. But there was a warmth in his grip, a knowing in his gaze, as though he sensed the unspoken desires I held inside. In that moment, I wanted his touch, his kiss, an intimacy I couldn't define. My uncle, the seafarer, had arrived in my life, and nothing would ever be the same.

But then reality broke the spell as he crossed the room. Each heavy footstep shattered my reverie like a stone hitting a fragile spider's web. The longing vanished, leaving an empty space behind—a harsh reminder that fantasies often remain fleeting wisps of thought, drifting like smoke.

He set his pack down in the corner without a word. Eager to welcome him, I switched on the dim light in my modest room. I glanced around, hoping to find something that might please him. But luck had deserted me, much like my last drops of sweet opium and fine wine. Then a thought struck: I noticed an old wine jar on the high shelf, a forgotten gift from the day I was born. It was just beyond reach. Undeterred, I clambered onto a stool, stretching until my fingertips could barely graze the cool glass. I paused to catch my breath.

Through a small window in the wall, my eyes were drawn outside to a captivating sight: in the desert beyond my room, beneath a towering cypress, sat an elderly man who looked remarkably like the monk I'd so often sketched. A young woman approached, extending a brilliant lotus blossom in her right hand. The old man seemed lost in thought, lightly biting the tip of his left index finger.

She slipped into the room as if by magic, her gaze wandering with quiet curiosity. A faint smile curved her lips, as though she was speaking to some invisible companion. Her eyes—those arresting Turkman eyes—showed both gentle reproach and irresistible pull. They danced with restless wonder, hinting at danger and delight in equal measure. I felt myself sink into their depths, drowning in the enigma of her soul.

Yet her beauty was more than just those eyes. High cheekbones, a broad forehead, and fine, arching eyebrows framed her face. Her lips, full and slightly parted, hinted at the memory of a tender kiss and the hope for another.

Moonlight shimmered over her body, revealing a tantalizing interplay of soft curves and strong lines. I was enthralled. Her back curved like a question, her hips answered it. The delicate features of her form contrasted with the firm muscles beneath, fueling my need to touch her.

She moved like a temple dancer, each gesture unfolding like a note in a seductive melody. So similar to the figure I'd painted so many times, she stirred something ancient and profound within me.

A black dress clung to her, demanding attention. I sensed she longed for the old man across the way, but something held her back. His laughter suddenly sliced the silence—cold, mocking. A chill pricked my skin as I noted his hollow face, his cruel smile.

Startled, I nearly dropped the wine bottle, my heart racing with both excitement and fear. My head spun. I placed the bottle down with trembling hands. When I looked up, the room stood empty; the old man's laugh faded into the night.

The space darkened, lit only by a flickering gaslight. A restless ache took root, telling me that nothing would ever be the same. One glance from that mysterious woman had altered my world.

She felt strangely familiar, as though we'd met in another life or in shared dreams. My heart burned with longing for her and the powerful bond I sensed between us. In a world so starved for genuine connection, all I wanted was her. But the echo of the old man's laughter lingered, a warning of the obstacle between us.

All through that dark night, my thoughts churned like a tempest, brimming with the urge to peer through the window in the wall. Yet his mocking laugh haunted me, fueling a fear that kept me from looking. As days blurred together, I wondered if her image would ever fade from my mind. Finally mustering my courage, I returned the wine bottle to its place.

Pulling aside the curtain, I faced an unyielding black wall, like a void swallowing my entire world. The window was gone, swallowed by the wall itself, as though it had never existed. I pounded on the spot under the weak glow of the gaslight, running my hands over the cold surface, but found no trace of any opening.

Her memory shaped me into a restless spirit, forever searching for proof of her reality. For two months and four days, I searched everywhere—every stone, every grain of sand—but uncovered no sign of the cypress, the water, or the footprints I so vividly recalled.

Over time, I realized she was unlike anyone else. The water for her swan's bath had to come from some secret source. Her clothing, woven by hands unseen, shone with a radiance beyond normal threads. Everything about her stood apart. The lotus flowers she offered were extraordinary. The thought of her brilliance diminishing under ordinary touch filled me with dread, as if the everyday world might tarnish her ethereal glow.

Wine and opium became my only respite, though they did little to muffle her memory. In fact, each passing day, hour, and minute sharpened the image of her face, making it more vivid and impossible to escape.

How could I erase her from my thoughts? Whether my eyes were closed or open, whether I was sleeping or awake, she lingered at the edge of my vision. Just as on that fateful night, she stood beyond the little window in my room, a window that once led to a world I was desperate to reach. Now, it was sealed off. She was lost to me—like a bouquet of bright flowers withering on barren soil.

A heavy, misty dusk wrapped itself around me, muting colors and blurring outlines. Yet in this foggy lull, I felt a curious sense of release. And then her image, so vivid and precise, emerged from the haze. Her still, unreadable face arrested my gaze like a haunting portrait.

The fog concealed my route home, but habit guided my steps to the door, where a dark silhouette sat unmoving. Lighting a match, I met a pair of wide black eyes—polite, observant, but seemingly hollow. Instantly, I knew it was her. I wanted to rouse her from that stillness, but my limbs felt anchored in place. The sting of the match burning my fingers jolted me back. I stepped aside. With quiet purpose, she rose and slipped into my dim home, eventually lying on my bed, her face in shadow.

She radiated a calm beauty unlike anything I'd seen. Her face, more remarkable than any I'd encountered, left me weak. Her dark eyes gleamed, reflecting a piece of my own life back at me, stirring something indescribably deep. I felt unsteady, as though the ground itself trembled beneath me. It was like surrendering—gentle as a lotus easing into restful sleep after an endless surge of waves.

My heart pounded, and I held my breath, terrified that the faintest noise might make her disappear like morning mist. A breathless hush stretched between us, as though sealed by glass. I felt trapped in that suspended instant, possibly forever. Her worn, fatigued gaze suggested she had witnessed something extraordinary—maybe even glimpsed death itself. As her eyelids lowered,

I quickly brushed the sweat from my brow with my sleeve.

She seemed pale and fragile in repose, a thin black dress outlining the length of her limbs. As I leaned closer, with her eyes still shut, the more I tried to approach, the further away she seemed. The secrets of her soul remained just beyond reach. She was like a distant star—a soft shimmer shedding faint light on the darkness of my life. I longed to break that silence, yet held back, frightened that any sound might disturb her, so used was she to otherworldly music.

Worried she might be hungry or thirsty, I hurried to my small pantry. Frantically, I checked the shelves for something she might find pleasing. I doubted my meager provisions would suit her refined palate, but I had to try. Then I spotted it: a dusty, long-forgotten bottle of wine, hidden on the top shelf since the day I was born. My pulse quickened as I carefully retrieved it, my hands unsteady. Returning to her side, I found her still lying there, like a worn-out child. Her dark lashes quivered against her cheeks, her breathing quiet and steady. Gingerly, I uncorked the bottle and lifted a cup to her slightly parted lips.

As the wine touched her mouth, I felt a deep peace wash over me. The endless torment and nightmares that had plagued me seemed, at last, to be loosening their grip. Sliding a stool closer, I studied her tranquil face. For the first time in what felt like a lifetime, a spark of hope glowed in my chest.

Innocence swathed in secrecy—no name could adequately capture her essence. Had her life been so private, so guarded? The heat radiating from her, and the faint scent of her dark hair, filled the room and drew me toward her.

My hand shook as if guided by a will beyond my own, reaching out to brush stray strands of hair from her temples. An immense curiosity gnawed at me: Who was she? What stories did she carry within? I yearned to unravel the many enigmas that surrounded her.

But as my fingers brushed her cold, damp hair, an icy shiver crawled up my spine. She was gone. I checked for a pulse, but found only silence. A mirror held to her lips showed no breath. Fear crashed over me like a wave.

A desperate need filled me—to warm her, to bring color back to her lifeless skin. Stripping off my clothes, I lay beside her, pulling her close. Her lips were bitter with opium; her body felt as cold as my dagger, but I held her anyway, hoping my warmth could spark a flicker of life.

Something about her drew me in. My hand trailed over her figure—the curve of her hips, the slope of her waist, the gentle rise of her chest. I held her tighter, trying to share my warmth. But a deep sorrow weighed on me, forcing me to pull away.

Rising from the bed, I felt the chill of the air remind me of my solitude. Each move I made to get dressed felt thick with meaning, a painful echo of what had just happened. She had changed me forever, and I sensed this was my fate: to bear her loss. It was a cruel irony—she had given me her body, but her soul had already slipped free. It seemed to drift up from her black dress, leaving me alone with what remained.

Her body would decay in time. Yet, in the darkness of my room, I discovered a strange unity with the universe through her stillness. My mind grew quiet, surrendering to a profound sense of belonging. Her eyes contained secrets, truths that compelled me to capture them.

We all return to what sustains us in moments of crisis: an addict to his drug, a writer to his pages, a sculptor to his clay. Such moments spark genuine creation. As a mere artist, I wondered if my humble craft could hold meaning.

I felt destined to paint her eyes. The urge intensified with each passing second. I lowered the gaslight. Its glow danced across her features, and I was determined to preserve her perfect stillness on paper.

Her face stirred something deep within me. I memorized her every contour, then closed my eyes and let my heart guide my hand. In the gentle sweep of lines and shadows, I found peace.

Serenity was my specialty, but this time her eyes were closed—did I need to see them again, or did their image already live in my mind? Time lost all meaning. I drew her face hour after hour, each attempt unable to fully capture the haunting beauty I craved. Then, with the first light of dawn, I found myself fixated on painting her eyes.

It was challenging. Memories of my past failures cluttered my mind, each brushstroke threatening to lose her essence. The harder I looked, the further she seemed to slip away. My efforts felt hopeless—until, in one startling instant, she changed. Her cheeks flared red, and her eyes—so alive, so filled with pain—snapped open, meeting my gaze. For a brief moment, she truly saw me. Then her lids fell shut again. But I had finally captured her expression, freezing that raw intensity. Approaching her, I realized she wasn't alive at all—my love had only sparked an illusion of life.

I drew closer, and the stench of rot assaulted me. Insects crawled across her skin, wasps buzzing with menace. She was gone. Had those open eyes been real or just my imagination? Her physical form mattered little now; soon it would feed the earth. I had captured her real essence in my drawing. From that moment on, I could summon her eyes whenever I wanted. Carefully, I tucked the sketch into my tin box, my secret trove.

What next? I couldn't leave her body. Burying her nearby, or dropping her into a well, felt dangerous. She was mine to claim, a trust given to me. A grim idea formed: I would dismember her, pack the pieces in my old suitcase, and bury it far away. My hand settled on the dagger's cold hilt, its blade flashing in the candlelight.

I worked with a determined calm, drawing the blade across her skin. The blood that oozed with each cut felt like a slow goodbye. With every limb I wrapped and placed in the suitcase, a deep reverence accompanied my detachment. When the job was done, I draped her black dress over the remains, then snapped the lock shut, the key clinking into my pocket.

Relief mingled with exhaustion. Lifting the suitcase, I marveled at its weight. Who was I now? The question haunted me, echoing in the silence.

Outside, a cold rain began to fall. Realizing I couldn't manage this alone, I stepped out and saw an old man huddled under a cypress, his face hidden by a ragged shawl. His chilling laughter made my skin crawl. "Need a porter?" he called out. "I'm your man. I ferry the dead to Sha'abdal Azim daily. Got coffins, all sizes, ready to go!"

My mouth opened to speak, but a knowing gleam in his eye stopped me. "No need to explain. I know your place. Come on, let's be off!" In one swift move, he stood. I guided him back to my room, where the suitcase waited.

Outside, a creaking hearse stood ready, drawn by horses that looked like living shadows. The old man climbed atop, whip in hand, his eyes fixed straight ahead. I wrestled the suitcase into the coffin space and lay down beside it.

He snapped the whip, and the horses lurched forward. Their hooves pounded the ground in a steady beat, bells jangling in a harsh counterpoint. The hearse rocked from side to side, its motion my only solace in that swirl of madness. The weight of the suitcase pressed against me, a grim reminder of what I'd done. We glided through fog-bound streets like ghosts, twisted trees and worn-down houses looming and vanishing in turn. The road coiled through skeletal branches and shadowed windows, all watching us in silent judgment.

The hearse jolted to a stop at the base of a mountain. "End of the line," the old man croaked, his voice like rusted metal. "Sha'abdal Azim's just around the bend. Not a better spot to lay your...load to rest."

Rounding a corner, I saw a secluded courtyard, ringed by lotus plants that absorbed the silence. I set down the suitcase, feeling some weight lift from my shoulders, though my heart still felt heavy. The old man's voice broke the hush: "Not even a bird ventures here. Good place for your business."

I reached for my pocket to pay, but only found copper coins. He laughed, a raspy sound. "No matter. I know where you live. I am a digger of graves, after all. Let's find the riverbed and finish up."

He hopped down with a lightness that startled me. "Follow me." We trudged to a dry riverbed near a tall cypress. "Here?" he asked, not waiting for my answer before he started digging. He tore into the ground like a dog after a bone. Soon, his shovel struck something hard. With one last heave, he pulled out a glazed pot, wrapped it in cloth, then stood and brushed off his hands. "Plenty of room left for your suitcase," he said, nodding at the hole. "Nobody'll find it here."

I tried to offer him the few coins I had, but he waved me off. "I've already been paid, courtesy of old Rey." He hefted the pot. "Have a nice day." And with that, he left me alone. I fit the suitcase into the hole and covered it with soil, piling lotus plants and stones on top until the suitcase all but disappeared.

By dusk, I caught sight of my blood-spattered clothes. I tried to wipe my face, but only smeared the stain. Insects buzzed around me—wasps and crawling worms. I brushed them off, a tremor rolling through me. Rain dripped as night fell, and I realized I held the reins of a funeral carriage, as though I'd inherited that old man's job. I felt hollow, as if I were drifting into a void. The memory of crimson-stained eyes clung to me, and peace felt impossibly distant. The only sound was leaves rustling. Exhaustion weighed me down, and my fear intensified.

I found myself in a graveyard, resting beside a headstone. A chilling laugh broke the silence, and I spotted a hunched figure next to me, cradling a pot. "You're lost," he hissed. "I'm the local gravedigger. Pulled this pot out of Rey's ruins. Take it." Instinct told me to pay, but he brushed off the idea. "I know where you live. Your carriage is ready."

He thrust the pot into my hands, and I trailed him to a waiting hearse. He limped up to the driver's seat, I climbed in after him, pot in my arms. He snapped the whip, and the horses moved on. Their hoofbeats soothed my nerves. Stars peered down on us, offering faint hope. The trees arched overhead, silhouettes merging in the dark. Houses glowed dimly, windows like vacant eyes, tree roots tangled around them. A stale odor of decay hung in the air, as though I'd been sealed in a coffin for eternity. I rode next to this ancient, stooped figure, his face hidden by the night.

We halted in front of my home. I stepped down and went inside with the pot. Setting it on the table, I retrieved a tin box from my bed, thinking to give it to the old man—but he was gone. When I unwrapped the pot, I saw its purple glaze shifting into gold, patterned with water lilies and bordered in blue.

Her face emerged on the pot, those black eyes staring back with an accusing gaze. Her features were wild—high cheekbones, wandering hair, a story in each line. It was undeniably her. I fished out an old sketch from the box. The likeness was uncanny, as if an unseen hand had guided me. The artwork on the pot shimmered, adding even more mystery, the eyes alive with a luminous depth. It felt too real.

I yearned to flee, yet how could I? Pain swelled again, and now two sets of eyes—mine on paper and the pot's—were locked on me. I felt trapped, but also strangely comforted. Whoever had painted this pot, centuries ago, must have known the same longing. Perhaps he, too, found himself haunted by those eyes. Our shared loneliness gave me a sense of solace, like a small light in the darkness.

Placing my sketch beside the pot, I set up a charcoal burner and watched flames spark to life. Drawing a few breaths of opium, I focused on those two faces until my worries eased. Under opium's soothing influence, my thoughts stretched into a dreamlike realm.

The burden on my chest lifted. It felt as if gravity released me, leaving me free to drift wherever my mind led. I floated on gentle waves of warmth, matching my heartbeat, blending with my pulse—wrapped in a calm embrace.

I longed to vanish into the silent void beyond sleep, to relinquish all sense of self. If only I could condense into a single note, a melody rising from ripples and outlines until I simply ceased to be. Slowly, my wish was granted. My heavy limbs melted into a languid fatigue, as though my existence was drifting away. Life ebbed, inviting old memories to resurface. I didn't merely recall them—I was transported to them, feeling younger by the moment.

Suddenly, everything blurred, and I fell into profound darkness. It was as if I teetered at the brink of an endless abyss, tethered by a single thread. Fragmented pieces of my past rose from oblivion. After what felt like a hush of pure emptiness, I found myself in a small, unfamiliar room, strangely welcoming in its obscurity.

As I wandered through these fleeting scenes, I sank deeper into the currents of my life. Each recollection, each feeling, wrapped around me, weaving me into a vast tapestry. This was the story I had yearned to unearth. Its clarity was so vivid that it felt like living it all over again.

I awoke in a strange but oddly familiar place, overwhelmed by a sense of déjà vu. It looked new to my eyes, yet resonated in my soul more powerfully than anything I'd known.

A lone gaslight flickered, its shadows dancing with the dread in my heart. I hovered in a realm between sleep and waking when a jarring sight snapped me alert: my robe and hands were smeared with blood. Shock and curiosity flared inside me, momentarily overriding my instinct to clean them.

Terror crept in as I imagined the villagers discovering my secret—their hushed gossip and suspicious glances. I hastily poured the last of my wine from a tarnished goblet, letting the liquid stain the floorboards.

An irresistible desire seized me: I needed to write, to make sense of my past. Drawing the gaslight closer, I let its glow fall across blank paper and began to write. The stillness of my room, which once sheltered me, broke under the scratch of my pen. At any moment, I expected the drunken guards to pound on my door, but I had no urge to run. Even if I could cleanse these bloodstains, I'd rather finish my wine than face their brutality. I needed to pour out my life's bitterness onto these pages—an offering to my own shadow. Was it a will? I owned nothing, had no soul worth saving. Still, I wrote because it was the only way to unburden myself, to reveal my truth. After I'm gone, someone might stumble upon these scribbled lines, but they'd never grasp the full depth of my darkness. It didn't matter; I wrote for the sake of writing, confessing to my shadow. It received my words with an understanding no living soul could match. In them, I laid bare the bitter dregs of my life. "This is all I had," I whispered.

Those who knew me in my younger days would scarcely recognize the bent old man I'd become: my back curved, my hair gone white, my eyes weighed down with unspoken tales. I dreaded meeting my own reflection, fearing the stranger I would find there. Yet the urge to share my story wouldn't relent. Where should I begin? Time has blurred the lines of memory. I'm tired of empty words. Every attempt to recount my history feels adrift, as though its authenticity were lost at sea.

My house stood over ancient ruins, echoing like a crypt. Small details mesmerized me for hours—a spider in the corner, a creaking floorboard. Since my universe shrank to this bed, the outside world had faded like a distant painting. A lone, rusty nail on the wall reminded me of better times when pictures of my wife and me hung there. Now the air smelled of sweat and stale breath, layered over the lingering scent of decay—a vivid tapestry of life's remains.

From this dimly lit room, I saw everything through two windows, both resembling empty frames. One overlooked our neglected yard, the other offered a glimpse of the city—a jumble of alleyways, time-worn houses, and lively bazaars. Even with my eyes closed, I sensed its shadows flickering in my mind. Once, its heartbeat matched my own; now it was a distant echo.

Across from me, a butcher shop stood out as a fixed point of routine. Every day, two sheep arrived, and the butcher—steady as the tides—performed his ritual. Two sleek black horses appeared each morning, their raspy breaths carrying down the alley. The butcher's hands gleamed with grease and henna as he prepared the carcasses, which swayed in slow arcs from his hooks. Once the horses left, the butcher, his grin as broad as it was disturbing, returned to his work. Even the bedraggled local stray, sporting a tattered yellow collar, peered up at him, head cocked to one side.

Further down the alley, an elderly man displayed his odds and ends on a sun-bleached carpet: sticks, horseshoes, gleaming beads, a rusty dagger, a mousetrap, a pencil sharpener, a chipped comb, a battered hoe, and a glazed pot concealed by a grimy rag. Cloaked in a threadbare shawl, cloak, and open vest, he sat hunched over his wares. Every Friday night, he recited from the Quran, his few remaining teeth gripping each verse like a lifeline. No one seemed to buy from him. His face, as familiar as a recurring dream, made me wonder what fills his pale head. At times, I had thought about approaching him—maybe purchasing some trifle—but my nerve always failed.

My nanny, Nonjoon, once told me tales about that old man living at the end of the street. She claimed he had been a potter who kept a single pot just for himself. Now, he ekes out a living selling these curios. In my mind, he's a gateway to a world beyond my confines—a world that only Nonjoon, my wife, and I share in secret.

Nonjoon, tall and strong as a tree, her hair the color of storm clouds, raised me from infancy. She cared for me and my wife—a woman rumored to have trysted with nearly every man in town, from the Quran reciter to the local philosopher, even the city's lawmen. I never knew my birth parents. Nonjoon filled that role, my only true family. Ironically, she was the one who arranged my marriage—to her own daughter.

Nonjoon's stories about my parents were rare and precious. One tale about my dad and his identical twin has stayed with me. They were mirror images, not just in looks but in personality too. So close, it seemed they shared every joy and sorrow, as if a single heart and soul fueled them both.

Both brothers, my father and uncle, were drawn to the colorful world of trade. In their early twenties, they set their sights on India, dealing in exotic goods like luxurious fabrics, fragrant shawls, and handmade pottery. My father made Varanasi his home, while my uncle traveled further, always seeking out new experiences in India's bustling markets.

Varanasi was a city of contrasts, its air thick with incense and its streets lined with holy rivers. My father felt an inexplicable pull, a call that drew him away from his business. The rhythmic beats of temple drums guided him until he stumbled upon a sacred place he hadn't meant to find. There, under the soft glow of temple lights, he saw her—Bogam Dasi. Her dance was a prayer, her movements graceful and her whole being dedicated to the Lingam shrine.

I pictured my mother, Bogam Dasi, as a vision of elegance. Her shimmering silk sari reflected the light, its folds moving in time with her dance. Her bare torso and gleaming hair framed her face, and her vibrant headband added a pop of color. I ached to touch her, to feel the warmth that radiates from her.

Her jewelry highlighted her beauty—jingling anklets, chiming bracelets, and a nose ring that sparkled like a sunbeam. Her large eyes were mesmerizing, just as they had been for my father. Her smile could light up a room, and her laughter was infectious. I imagined her dancing to the music of the sitar, tombak, tambour, cymbals, and karna, her body telling a story, her movements drawing in every watcher.

How can I, a son who never knew his mother, capture her essence? I focus on the memory of her, not out of desire but out of a need to understand her. I imagine feeling her touch, not in a prurient way but as a way to connect with her grace. Those who don't get this just don't get the depth of human connection.

My longing is part of a larger story of desire that goes back generations. My father must have felt the same pull. He was swept up in Bogam Dasi's dance, surrounded by the scents of mogra and sandalwood. Their moments together were full of soft words and intense looks, a bond so strong he adopted her Lingam faith.

Picture them under India's star-studded sky, suspended between earthly passion and the cosmic dance. There, bathed in the soft glow of lanterns, he traced her silhouette as if sketching constellations, their heartbeats merging into the universal rhythm. With eyes brimming with unspoken poetry, they locked gazes, succumbing to a moment that foretold my coming.

While my father was away on long sea trips to India, my uncle occasionally stepped in, supposedly to help. But my mother, alone in her isolation, craved more than just money; she longed for a deeper bond. Yet, it wasn't just about emotional closeness. The allure of intimacy intrigued her anew, as my father had been her only lover. How could she ignore the desire for the rough touch of a hand or the gentle trace of a tongue on her thigh? In such fragile moments, one can easily be drawn into the excitement of the unknown. My mother, once shunned by her spiritual brethren, found herself caught in the web of affection my uncle spun. Trapped between two reflections of the same face, she faced a tangled dilemma: was she merely a pawn in my uncle's game, or did she truly enjoy the attention from two lovers? She yearned for a man of unyielding courage, so Bogam-Dasi devised the Rite of the Serpent—a harrowing gauntlet of valor. The trial would pit my father and uncle in a room with a deadly cobra, a reptile ruled by its lethal instincts. The first to utter a scream would cue the snake charmer to rescue the other. To the last man standing, Bogam-Dasi vowed her fidelity.

Before my father faced his fate, he asked Bogam-Dasi for a final dance in the temple. Her movements were mesmerizing, like the cobra they were about to face. With the last note still in the air, the lovers were led into a dark chamber—the cobra's lair.
The air grew heavy; silence fell, making it hard to speak. Then, a laugh echoed off the walls. It felt like death itself reveled, feeding off their fear.

Finally, the door opened, and my uncle came out, a shadow in the dim light. His hair had turned white; his eyes looked empty, as if he had stared into the abyss. Mistaken for my father, he was shunned. His experience cast a shadow over my life. From then on, I was a child known but not loved. The man they mistook for my father—uncle or father, it no longer mattered—moved to Rey for work, taking Bogam-Dasi with him.

Before they left, my mother handed Nonjoon a jug of red wine, laced with cobra venom. A token from her own love story. In that potent wine, I found echoes of my mother's past, in every bitter sip. Maybe my mom was still out there, dancing in some town, lit by torches, her movements hypnotic. It was as if the snake's venom courses through her, mesmerizing the crowd. Maybe my dad, or my uncle with his white hair, watched from the shadows, memories of the dark room rushing back. The cobra's hiss and dance, its cold gaze and deadly venom—as potent as the wine—still linger.

My story isn't the idyllic tale you might imagine. I was raised by Nonjoon, the towering lady with gray wisps in her hair, right in this very house alongside her daughter, my wife. As far back as I remember, Nonjoon was like a mother to me, and I loved her deeply. So when the time came, I married her daughter, my childhood companion, my wife. She was so much like her mother. One moment with her, beside Nonjoon's body, is forever etched in my mind.

I crept into the dim room where Nonjoon lay, the flickering light of camphor candles casting shadows. A Quran rested on her chest, a shield for her soul. Gently lifting the veil from her face, I saw her at peace. The sight forced me to face death's presence—so real yet profound, like a newborn's first cry. A tiny smile played on her lips, as if she took a secret with her. I meant to kiss her hand goodbye, but then, her daughter stepped into the room. She leaned into me, her lips finding mine. Shame and desire swirled inside me, mixing like oil and water. It felt like Nonjoon's own laughter echoed through the room, a knowing chuckle that saw through our flaws. Even the Quran's verses faded, overshadowed by the pull of desire. I couldn't resist, I kissed her back. Just then, the curtain to the next room swept open. Her father appeared, hunched, a shawl draped around his neck.

He started laughing, a dry laugh that sent a shiver down my back. His shoulders shook with every laugh, but he didn't look my way. Shame surged through me, so intense I wished the earth would swallow me whole. What a mess! I rushed out, wondering if she set this up to trap me into marriage.

Though we were raised as siblings, I was pushed into marrying her, to save her family's honor. I didn't know any of this firsthand; it was all rumors. On our wedding night, she was like an elusive bird, flinching at my touch. My gentle words only drove her away. "I am tarnished," she whispered, her voice fragile. It was as if she feared me. The lights dimmed, and she huddled in the corner, lost in her shame. Our connection was severed. The nights passed, and I felt more estranged.

A line was drawn, and I dared not cross it. So, on the cold floor, on her side of the room, I slept. Can you imagine? For two months and four days, I was an outcast in my own marriage, banished to the floor, afraid to go near her.

Rumors whispered of her wild days, her craving for freedom. Her taste in men? A mystery I couldn't solve. The foolish, the clueless, the ones oblivious to the world's reality—they were drawn to her like dogs scenting meat outside the butcher's shop. Yet, it was she whom they pursued. I've watched them, smirking, winking, their laughter a stinging burn in my chest. I'd forced a smile, feigning indifference, trying to regain respect, if not from her, then from the crowd.

That night, I found the courage to face her, to pierce the armor of her enigma. The air was heavy, not with words, but with unspoken doubts, with the question: am I just another foolish dog, or something more?

But when I finally found my voice, she was gone. The room was hollow, echoing with her absence. In the quiet of the night, I sought solace in her empty bed, in the lingering warmth, the scent of her like fading smoke. It lulled me to sleep, but even dreams betrayed me, leaving me to wake in a chill that had nothing to do with the cold.

Every homecoming echoed with her absence,

a void that gnawed at my soul. Each time our eyes met, hers were cold, distant, a reminder of the puzzle I couldn't solve, the gap I couldn't bridge. Had I been too cautious, too afraid to truly reach for her? Was it my own doubts that pushed her away?

I felt the pull of the wild crowd she fell in with, the ones who shared her nights. I saw her laughing with a wine seller, his eyes crinkling at the corners, and later, deeply engaged in conversation with a Quran reciter, his voice a soothing hum. From watchful guards to aimless youth, from deep thinkers to simple minds, each was an oddity, never quite touching the core of love. But she found joy among these defiant characters, while I merely watched from a distance. They knew her in ways I didn't, understood some hidden part of her soul.

I mocked myself for fearing loss of a connection I'd never had. I tried to fit into their world, to uncover her secret charm. I tried to match their strides, but felt like an outsider. I caught her eye, but saw only distance, a quiet echo of my fears.

Her charm was wild, complex—a flicker in her eye, a note in her laugh. Loving her was deeper than what most could imagine. Was it her beauty, the secret world she held, or a childhood love I still felt? I couldn't tell. Only that she'd carved a deep yearning within me. I longed to touch her, feel her pulse, connect our souls far from the noise of the world.

In the room's dim corner, my gaze locked onto the elegant curve of her legs. At first, I thought shadows played tricks on my eyes. But then, clearer, more real, they emerged—demonic beings. They resembled human-like genies, their bodies inscribed with divine verses, wrapping around her thighs. One seemed to embody wild passion, another shone with the promise of wealth. Their presence was mesmerizing, holding my gaze captive. Each touch lit a fire in her eyes, a blaze of longing and temptation.

Witnessing this, I felt an ache of defeat wash over me, more intense than ever before. The bitter truth had seeped into my soul, drenching my heart with a mix of hatred and a thirst for revenge. She was drawn to fleeting desires, things I could never fully grasp or compete with. I yearned to offer her my enduring love and true devotion, but she favored the temporary highs found in others. The thought of spending just one night with her was eating away at me from the inside.

She seemed to take pleasure in my pain, like pouring salt into a fresh wound. Gradually, I felt myself fading away into a shadow of the man I once was. My body was confined to these four walls, yet my thoughts roamed aimlessly, unable to escape. Our union, a marriage where love only flowed one way, eroded my spirit with each passing day.

Even my loyal nurse, who had witnessed my decline, faulted me for not being the man my wife desired. Her words hurt, but they seemed trivial compared to the rumors swirling around town.

The gossip had it that no woman should be stuck with a man as naïve and utterly devoid of allure as myself. And, as much as I hated to admit it, a part of me couldn't help but agree.

Every night, I'd look in the mirror, barely recognizing the face staring back at me. I was worn, faded, almost a stranger to myself. Crawling into bed, I found no solace, my gaze locking onto the blank wall across the room. A whirlpool of darkness drew me in, fears and sorrows swirling, parting like a curtain to reveal long-buried desires crying out to be heard. I felt cut off from the world of the living, standing at the edge of an endless void.

A whisper would break the silence: "Death, where are you?" These words brought a fragile sense of peace, like mist descending onto a troubled sea. It eased me into a restless quiet, a deceptive calm that cradled my thoughts for a heartbeat or two. But just as I began to let go, reality snapped back into focus, as if yanked by a puppeteer's string. I found myself in the center of the town square, the shadow of the gallows stretching over me like a dark omen. A twisted old man dangled from the rope, his face warped into a grotesque grin.

The scene was bizarre—townsfolk milled around as if at a fair, some even raising glasses of wine in a toast. Then I saw her—Nonjoon. Her eyes blazed with the same fiery anger I'd seen in my wife during our fiercest fights. She led me through the crowd, pointing toward a figure draped in blood-red robes. She leaned close, her voice tinged with menace, "You're next."

My eyes snapped open, my body slick with cold sweat, my heart thundering as if I'd barely evaded the Grim Reaper's deadly scythe. I gulped down water, splashed my face, desperate to banish the nightmare and find sleep once more. But sleep proved elusive, a taunting mirage that receded with the deepening night.

Tangled in my sheets, sleep seemed within reach yet always danced just out of grasp. The stern face of Nonjoon invaded my thoughts, shattering my fragile peace. Even swaddled in my bed's warmth, my hands felt icy, not with cold but with the dread that had taken hold of my soul.

I heard Nonjoon's footsteps outside my door. She was probably out procuring fresh bread and cheese for breakfast. A street vendor's call drifted through the window, a reminder that day had broken, as a sunbeam slipped in, painting patterns on the ceiling.

The nightmare began to recede, sinking into the depths of my mind like a forgotten fear. Nonjoon entered, her tray bearing the usual morning fare. But today, her face seemed different, as if she carried a secret burden of thoughts.

Nonjoon had always been an enigma. Lately, she seemed lost in her own world, one I couldn't decipher. She savored life's simple joys, yet a shadow of concern for the future seemed to cling to her. For me, life raced by, each day as dense as a year. And in that moment, it struck me: we often appreciate life's value only when reminded of its fleeting nature.

As the day wore on, the room grew increasingly oppressive. I was drenched in sweat, my skin glowing in the dim light. My tired, blurry eyes struggled to focus on the empty ceiling. Even breathing felt like a chore, as if the air had grown heavier. When Nonjoon entered with a meal, I startled so badly that I shrieked. The sound seemed to rouse every dark corner of the room, sending even a stray cat scurrying.

In the ensuing chaos, a voice rang out, a cry for help that almost brought a smile to my lips. Soon, a doctor appeared, a solid man with a wise-looking beard. "How about some opium?" he suggested. It sounded mad, but once I took it, my foggy mind cleared. My thoughts sharpened, as if exploring a thrilling new world. I felt weightless, free, unjudged.

I gazed out the window to see Nonjoon in the yard, bathed in the gentle afternoon sun. Her long shadow fell on the courtyard wall. She had been conversing with a prostitute, my wife, for some time. Though they tried to conceal it, I could easily read lips. I possessed skills that the foolish people around me, including Nonjoon and the woman, not only lacked but were oblivious to. Their words were clear as day: "We have lost hope; only God can help him now." It was evident the doctor had divulged my condition.

I couldn't help but wonder—why the act? Why pretend to care about me? Nonjoon wasn't getting paid, so what was she after? Was her concern genuine, her affection true, or was this all just a ploy to use me? I had no answers, but one thing was certain—Nonjoon had become a lifeline. Her presence over the years had brought me a sense of peace.

Nonjoon was more than just a caregiver—she'd looked after me like family. She'd bring me food, nurse me back to health when I was ill. Her face would crease with worry, and every day she'd open up about her life as if I were an old friend. I never grew tired of her stories.

But there was something odd about the way Nonjoon spoke of her daughter-in-law. It wasn't idle gossip—whenever she mentioned the woman, a change would come over her. Her voice would shift, taking on a haunted quality that sent a shiver down my spine. There was a pull to her words, a hint of secrets untold, of a painful past she kept at bay. Guilt hung heavy in her voice, as if she walked a tightrope, careful not to reveal too much. And when she prayed... it was as if she pleaded for forgiveness, begged God to keep her secrets locked away. Sometimes tears would stream down her face, but she never spoke of the pain that drove her to cry. It was as if she wrestled with a darkness that refused to be vanquished.

I never got religion. The idea of faith, of believing in something you can't see or touch? It seemed like a mass delusion, each person conjuring their own God. I'd gone through the motions, prayed at the mosque, recited the Quran, but it never felt real. Now, stuck in my room, it all seemed like a bad joke. Nonjoon's prayers hadn't changed a thing – I only got sicker. Would I even live to see the sun again?

It was those useless prayers during times of suffering that made me question faith. Were people true believers or just scared? To me, faith seemed like a comforting lie, a way to escape the harsh truth. When death stared them in the face, all the rituals and prayers meant nothing. None of it brought comfort. That's when religion seemed like nothing more than empty promises.

These thoughts filled me with a dread I couldn't shake. It's something you can't understand unless you've been there. My longing for life grew so strong that any moment of joy could overshadow the fear of what lay ahead.

I felt like a ghost, forgotten by those around me. Stuck in a place between life and death, cut off from the world. One evening, I gazed out the window. A lone tree stood in the shadows, its image blurring with the closed butcher shop. The fading light made everything seem temporary, as if it could disappear any moment. The dark sky above twinkled with stars. The melancholy call to prayer broke the silence, a mournful sound amidst the shadows. A stray dog's whimper echoed through the night, a lonely cry that matched my own isolation.

"I guess my guiding star is barely shining at all," I thought to myself.

Then, laughter and voices filled the alley. Drunken men sang joyfully:

"Come on, let's party!
Let's drink some of that good Rey wine,

If not now, then when?"

Their laughter faded into the night, leaving me alone in the darkness. I fought the urge to light my lamp, finding comfort in the shadows that seemed to hold my deepest fears.

A figure sat in the dimness, its face expressionless. It stirred memories of the butcher from my childhood. Each time I looked away, I felt its penetrating gaze. This figure, hauntingly familiar, seemed like a ghost from my past. When I lit the lamp, the figure vanished. In the mirror, I saw a stranger. I was a shadow of my former self. My own voice broke the silence, whispering "Death... death..." The word hung in the air, contrasting with the stillness. In that moment, I felt like a fall leaf, delicate and directionless, suspended in a final dance.

Sleep pulled me in, into a vivid dream world. Memories swirled together in a tapestry of shadows and light. This world felt more real than my waking life. The dream lingered, challenging my reality.

I walked through a twisted cityscape. Buildings rose in alien shapes – pyramids, cones, cubes. The air held a silent tragedy; the inhabitants were desiccated shells, marked by twin rivulets of blood.

I came to the butcher's shop, the shopkeeper familiar. His head rolled to the floor, and panic seized me. I ran through the alleys, finding more victims. I didn't dare look back, fearing what might follow.

The dream shifted. I stood before my father-in-law's home, a place of safety. My brother-in-law sat in sunlight, a contrast to the darkness. I offered him pastries, but his head detached at my touch. I woke with a scream, my heart racing.

As I caught my breath, I heard the soft creak of the door. Nonjoon had arrived to clean and set my meal by the window. From this attic vantage point, the old man who usually lingered near my room was hidden from view. Instead, my gaze fell upon the butcher. His movements were deliberate, as if trapped in the rhythm of his work. The only sound was the occasional cough of the dark horses outside, each carrying a sheep.I found myself mesmerized by the butcher. His hand, slick and sure, wiped his apron before lifting two sheep onto hooks. His fingers moved with precision over the sheep's thighs, each stroke practiced and exact. It was as if he knew every contour, every hidden vessel.As I watched the butcher carve the meat, a strange thought seized me. I wondered if his wife's skin was as tender as the flesh he cut with such skill. Was her touch as smooth as silk, her appeal as intoxicating as a moonless night full of secrets?This idea conjured a vivid image of her. Her body was a tapestry of gentle curves and shadowed hollows. Her clothes seemed to whisper stories of hidden longings, inviting further exploration. A bold notion emerged: could the butcher, with his skilled hands, elevate her beauty to an art form? What culinary creations could her form inspire? Each feature - her cheeks, her tongue, her limbs, her breasts - a potential ingredient in a tale of flavors.As I indulged in these fantasies, my hand instinctively went to the hidden knife in my chest pocket. I carefully drew it out, cleaned the blade on my robe, and returned it to its hiding place. The butcher's dance between life and death had sparked a long-dormant hunger within me. I was consumed by an insatiable desire to explore this forbidden realm.I turned my attention back to the window. A single patch of blue sky peeked out from behind thick, ominous clouds. It seemed impossibly far away, as if only an endless ladder could reach it. The sky was heavy with yellowish clouds, weighing down the city, thickening the air with unspoken tension. In such weather, thoughts of death were inescapable.

Yet, as its shadow loomed over me, my determination only hardened.

Just then, a funeral procession moved past my window. The coffin was covered in black cloth with a lone candle flickering atop it. The chant of "Beyond the veil, we yield," broke through my thoughts. Even the butcher stepped away from his work to honor the dead. The elderly vendor, however, remained still, untouched by the solemnity. Faces in the crowd seemed lost in thought, as if pondering the eternal mystery of what comes after. Nonjoon looked anxious, murmuring prayers as she backed out of my room to continue her solemn chants.

In a world where connecting with the living often felt like a burden, these moments of ritual brought me a strange comfort. My room felt like a sanctuary of solitude, a tomb even colder than the graves below. I often wondered, is this how the dead feel, enclosed in their final resting place?

Once life leaves us, what happens to our essence? Do our thoughts and feelings just vanish, or do they linger, unresolved, in the depths of our being? I've pondered over death so much that the fear has dissipated, replaced by a strange desire for the unknown. The only dread remaining is that my essence might mingle with those I deem unworthy, a thought too unbearable to entertain.

I've found myself at times feeling like I am at the edge of life, almost stepping into another realm. Having separated myself from the world and its relentless cravings, a tranquility had settled over me. What remains is a simple curiosity about what comes next. The here and now, filled with ceaseless desires and endless striving, often felt exhausting. If another life awaited, might it promise a simpler, more serene experience, far removed from this world's chaos?

Death seems to promise something that life never could—a final stillness, a complete peace. It beckons us towards an existence free from the puppet strings of life, a realm where the soul might finally find its eternal rest.

Where life is a dizzying fair, crowded with hollow noises, death is the quiet river, calmly flowing towards the boundless ocean. This tranquility isn't bleak but brimming with a strange allure. It's in death's embrace that the spirit finds its ultimate release. This dichotomy between life's cluttered canvases and death's pristine tranquility casts a profound silhouette, making the silent visitor more enticing than the grand charade of existence. And throughout our journey, it's death that sings to us. Hasn't everyone, at some point, been caught in a deep, unexplainable self-reflection, lost to time and space, unaware of their own thoughts? Then, they have to gather their strength to come back to their outside world and reality; this is the siren song of death.

Lying on my damp, clinging sheets, my eyelids grew heavy with the weight of impending sleep. It was a gateway, not to peace, but to a torrent of suppressed memories and unfounded fears that chose this moment to awaken. The irrational terrors began to parade before me: the notion of pillow feathers morphing into slicing blades, an ordinary shirt button ballooning into the cumbersome weight of a millstone, and the bizarre thought of a simple piece of flatbread shattering like thin ice upon the kitchen tiles.

As the night deepened, my fears magnified. The mundane became monstrous—an unattended gaslight teetered precariously in my mind, its fall capable of igniting a firestorm that could devour the city. A dog's bark, ragged and rough outside the nearby butcher's shop, twisted into the sound of a horse's desperate whinny.

My room transformed into a stage for grotesque visions: an old man with a pig's snout for a nose cackled madly at his own jokes, his laughter echoing unchecked. A harmless worm wriggling in the sink morphed in the shadows, threatening to become a venomous snake. The bed beneath me, once a place of rest, now seemed a tombstone ready to entomb me, sliding over my body with the finality of a grave sealed by the rockslide of a tomb.

The silence around me grew oppressive, filled with the echo of my own stifled screams, as I called out into the void with no hope of an answer. Each image, each sound, and each fear spun together, weaving a tapestry of the night that held me captive in its chilling embrace.

I longed to return to the simplicity of my childhood, yet when I revisited those memories, they came marred by harsh realities. Memories now carried the echoes of coughs that reminded me of the frail, black horses outside the butcher's shop. The fear of spitting out blood—a vital, salty life-force, reluctantly expelled—lingered hauntingly. The ever-present shadow of mortality colored every thought, leaving no respite, only a pervasive sadness and dread.

Throughout life, we craft masks, shaping them quietly, with detachment, as if they are mere tools for survival. Some cling to one mask until it is frayed and soiled, revealing their opportunistic nature. Others save their masks for special events, while some continuously change theirs, only to find that their last mask is threadbare, its charm lost, revealing the true face behind it.

This game of pretense isn't just about how we interact with others; it echoes through the winding corridors of our self-perception, shaped ceaselessly, yet subtly, by the surrounding world. This influence is so understated that it leads me to wonder about the quiet, unseen power my room's walls hold over my mind. The room itself seems haunted, perhaps by the ghost of a madman once confined within, or maybe a hardened criminal.

Even beyond these lifeless barriers, the influence extends. The butcher skillfully carving meat, the old man with his disturbing laugh, my ever-watchful nursemaid, the unsettling faces I encounter, the food that sustains me, and the clothes I wear—all subtly weave into the fabric of my thoughts, molding them in silent conspiracy.

One night, in the bathhouse, as I stood under the cascade of warm water, forgotten memories bubbled up. The attendant showered me, each splash washing away layers of my muddled thoughts. Steam filled the room, and in it, my reflection seemed as fragile as it had been a decade ago, back in the days of my youth. The outline of my body, projected onto the misty walls, triggered a rush of memories, shading the curves of my thighs, calves, and waist with a poignant sensuality.

The attendant's hands, steady and experienced, moved over my skin with the ease of a butcher expertly slicing through a sheep's thigh. His touch, both solid and precise, danced a delicate ballet over my form. His worn hands, seasoned by years of work, found a natural rhythm, smoothing out the tense knots hidden beneath my skin. As his fingers traced further, exploring every contour, a quiet intimacy unfolded in the steam-filled air, sketching a silent story of vulnerability mingled with control.

Around me, the shadows of other bathers loomed large and commanding, stark against the bathhouse walls, their presence overpowering and enduring. In contrast, my own shadow seemed to flicker and fade too quickly. As I dressed, the atmosphere shifted, as if I were crossing into a different realm. It felt like emerging into a reality less welcoming, yet within me, life stirred anew, impressively resilient, as though I had not just dissolved like a cube of salt in the bathhouse waters.

"I lived," I reflected, caught in a surreal mesh of existence. My life, as peculiar and elusive as the intricate design on the pen case I now used for writing. An artist, absorbed in their craft, must have etched this pattern. I find myself continuously drawn to it; it strangely feels like home. Perhaps this design is what inspires my words.

The pattern depicts a tall cypress tree under which an old man sits, reminiscent of an Indian yogi. He is clad in a robe, a shawl wrapped around his head, his left index finger pressed to his lips as if arrested by a sudden revelation. Opposite him, a young girl in a flowing black dress spins in a dance that sends shivers down the spine. She might be a Bogam Dasi, a lotus flower delicately held in her hand, a slender stream flowing between them, marking a gentle but undeniable separation.

Seated on the edge of the opium rug, my dark thoughts dissolve into the swirls of smoke. The opium gently lifts me into a realm filled with vivid colors and deep mysteries. Wrapped in a robe near the glowing tray, I see the old man with his distinctive beard in the rug, laughing in a way that fills the air. His laughter, rich and unsettling, sends a shiver down my spine.

I rise, letting the robe fall to the floor, and walk toward the mirror. My cheeks are flushed, my skin pale, reflecting the light like the cuts in a butcher's display. My beard is wild, framing a face that carries the marks of weariness yet holds a subtle depth. My eyes, though tired, retain a trace of innocence, touched by a quiet sorrow. As I look at myself, there's an unexpected allure in this moment of raw exposure. I think to myself, "Your sadness has touched your eyes... Would tears, if they came, emerge from such depth, or not at all?"

A wave of revulsion washes over me as I lock eyes with my own reflection. "Fool," I mutter, the word slicing through the silence. "Why sink into this sorrow?" My gaze scours the room, desperate for a distraction. Perhaps a hidden bottle of wine could soften the jagged edges of my thoughts.

As the room begins to tilt, a slow, dizzying spiral, my voice sounds distant, echoing in the cavern of my skull. My hands feel bulky and cumbersome at my sides; my eyelids are heavy, dragging down; my lips are thick and numb. There, reflected in the glass, I watch myself slowly fade into the opium's foggy embrace, the world around me blurring into shadows.

As the opium's gentle haze was about to envelop me, Nonjoon appeared in the doorway. A laugh burst from me, deep and rich. Her face, though, remained a blank canvas—her eyes hollow, her expression impenetrable, betraying no hint of surprise, anger, or sorrow.

This laughter wasn't just an outburst at the absurd; it was a rich echo of life's enigmatic twists, wrapped in the stillness of the night—a testament to human folly. Without a word, Nonjoon quietly collected the heated tray and slipped away.

Sweat beaded on my forehead; I wiped it away and noticed my palms dotted with white. I leaned back against the wall, pressing my head to the cold, hard bricks, finding a faint relief. Then, almost without thinking, a song began to weave itself through the quiet:

"Come on, let's party!
Let's drink some of that good Rey wine,
If not now, then when?"

A strange weight pressed on my chest, like the quiet before a storm, drawing me into a wild, unknown world.

Fear gripped me, mingling with the deep sadness that sapped my energy. At my room's entrance, the scruffy old man and the butcher lingered, their presence casting a shadow. Their silent forms by the doorway stirred a quickened pulse, weaving threads of wariness through my thoughts.

Nonjoon once told me a story that still haunts me. She insisted, her voice serious as she swore on the Prophet, that a disheveled old man had been sneaking into my wife's room late at night. She even heard my wife whisper to him, urging him to loosen his shawl. Soon after, I saw something unsettling: the imprint of the old man's dirty, decaying teeth on my wife's lips, a stark contrast to the sacred verses she recited from the Quran. Those holy words seemed to darken, becoming twisted as they touched my wife's lips. Was it possible that she had enticed this troubled soul to her?

Compelled by a strange curiosity later that day, I approached the old man's market stall to ask about a jug's price. His reply was a hoarse, eerie laugh that showed off his decayed, stained teeth, making me uneasy. "You're going to buy it without looking? This jug is worthless, lad, just take it!" Despite my confusion, I laid down two Qiran and four Abbasi on the edge of his tablecloth. His laugh echoed once more, this time sending a cold wave over me. Feeling a desperate need to escape, I covered my face with my hands and quickly left.

The old man's stall was a cavern of rust and decay, each scent a stark reminder of time's relentless erosion. His wares, as worn and tired as his own bent frame, seemed like fragments from a forgotten chapter of life.

Despite the dust and neglect, these items vibrated with a subtle life force, each piece quietly resonating with echoes of its former days. Their silent stories reached me, stirring deeper feelings than any conversation with the living could evoke.

Then Nonjoon arrived with unsettling news that spread like a cold draft through the marketplace. She recounted tales of my wife's secret liaisons with a mysterious intruder, claiming their bed had become a haven for lice while she lingered in her baths. The image of the man's shadow, perhaps slick with sweat, looming against the bathhouse wall haunted me—a shadow driven by lust, feeding on its own corrupt desires.

Yet, strangely, I found myself not seized by rage. This man was no ordinary adulterer; he was not one of those bland deceivers who ensnare the unwary. There was something distinct about him, a tragic quality that marked him as a man overshadowed by his own griefs, a solemn figure cast against the stark realities of life.

The marks of his yellow, decaying teeth on my wife's lips—where once she whispered holy verses—were clear. My wife, who now denied me even the simplest affection and mocked my longing, still held a piece of my heart. Despite her dismissals, I found myself yearning for the faintest touch of her lips.

The day was bathed in a glaring yellow light. A woodpecker's call shrieked into the distance, reminding me of vulnerability and unearthing old, gloomy phobias within myself. The kind of trouble that used to disturb my peace was approaching in the offing and I readied myself for its homecoming. It felt as if there were a fever smothering me, holding me tight on its relentless grip; I could imagine myself suffocating. So I staggered towards the bed and closed my eyes down. My clothes pinched me like a vice; so I sat up in my madness moaning "...Too much...too much" Suddenly, I became silent as my mind raced through the stormy thoughts within it. Then with an ironic smile on my faceless lips, I whispered "Stop...what a dupe I have been". These words echoed around the room not to be understood but just tore through the stifling silence trying to fill this yawning desolation.

After a while, out of the blue, the door fell wide open and she entered the room like an explosion of sunlight. She clearly remembered me sometimes; I took what relief I could from that. She knew about my agony, how I was disappearing little by little into nothingness. But there was something I still needed to know: did it ever occur to her that all this time it's been her not being here which has destroyed me? If only she had—then I might die contented and be the most joyful dying person who ever lived.

My thoughts were illuminated by her being there. I couldn't quite tell what it was – maybe the delicate halo that enveloped her, or the way she moved so gently – that eased my pain. But this time, she looked healthier. She seemed surer of herself. She had taken care in getting ready; she wore a sleek taupe dress that matched her well-groomed brows and lightly made up face. It was like a lightbulb went off in my head when I saw her looking like this – she had always been beautiful and graceful, but now it seemed different somehow.

Her face was at peace, which is strange because it seemed like she should've been angry. I'd always wondered that about her. Was this the same girl who used to wear black pleated skirts and run around with me by the river? Was this the girl who once made my heart skip a beat with just a glimpse of her ankle beneath her dress? I guess I never really thought about it until now, like I'm seeing her for the first time through a veil.

I didn't know why, but all of a sudden I pictured sheep on their way to be slaughtered outside of a butcher shop. She had become utilitarian to me in certain ways: the parts of her that had intrigued me were overshadowed by what she did for me or could do for me. Somewhere along the line, she grew into a woman who thought before she spoke and considered where she was going in life, while I stayed fifteen years old—stuck right there on that bench in front of all those trees.

Her change was so awkward that I became ashamed. I felt as if she had become open to all except me, and all I could do was hold on to the memories of her youth.

What I wanted most was that old, innocent expression which spoke of nothing but purity—the one she wore before time sketched its tales of experience around her eyes. She wasn't who she used to be.

She didn't care at all when she asked, "How are you feeling?" So my answer was just as harsh, "You're living freely aren't you? Doing whatever you want? Then why should you care about my health?"

She left quickly, and the door closed with a loud noise. But she did not look back. She went away like the shock of cold that makes you realize you are lonely. I wanted to run after her, and cry at her feet, and beg her pardon.

I thought that if only I could weep I might get some relief. There was something rather pleasant in having a bone or two broken at last; one got out of the ruck of the daily round. It was big enough to lift me above humanity altogether, beyond heaven almost.

I felt like I was on top of the world for a second there. It was like I had ascended, been touched by God himself...

And then she came back. She wasn't as cold-hearted as I thought. Overwhelmed by guilt, I knelt before her and cried until time seemed to stop. When my tears finally stopped falling, she was gone. Suddenly, every emotion I've ever felt hit me all at once and three times as hard. It was like coming back to a place you haven't been in years—a place where an old man with his pig sits next to a burning tar-filled rug and watches smoke curl into the sky.

Everything stood still while the smoke rose. That black, thick smoke wrapped around my skin, stained my hands and face. Nonjoon walked in with a tray of barley soup and chicken with turnips; she froze when she saw me. Off the walls bounced her scream as she dropped the tray and ran from the room. A sick part of me loved how terrified I had made her feel.

I woke up and turned off the gas lamp next to my bed before going to look in the mirror. The monster that stared back at me from the glass sent a chill down my spine. I used my hands to twist my features into odd, frightening shapes. There were countless faces inside me now, all demanding to come out. Each of these visages was strange; they were mine but seemed so foreign, changing at even the slightest contact with them. In one face there was an old man's visage; in another it belonged to the butcher or my wife, yet none of them were really mine.

Were my face a mirror of tacit suffering and anonymous woe, silent for duty and inherited for griefs? Without my knowledge, did I let them out—swinging between mad delirium and raptured glee as they do in my countenance? Only by death could it rest!

But would these masks that I had worn have left behind some signs? In one single instant I understood what I was doing and what it might signify. A laugh!—but such a laugh—oh God!—as never came from me before. Then there was a weight on my chest—I coughed—a great clot of blood flew against the looking-glass; I wiped it off with my hand, and left a bloody smudge upon the glass. Turning round, there stood my nurse in the moonlight—the very soup-bowl clutched in her hands, barley-soup which she had brought for me—her face white as a sheet, her hair all wild about her head, her eyes staring open with terror. So I hid my face in shame behind the curtain.

I was lying in bed and trying to sleep, but my head felt like it was on fire. I'd poured sandalwood oil into the lamp and now the smell of it was everywhere—filling my nose, choking me. I could smell her feet through the sheets: sour-sweet sweat; the taste of opium clung to my tongue from her mouth. My hand moved over my body, feeling for the shape of my limbs against hers, pale copies—her calves, thighs, arms. The roundness of her thigh pressed itself against me; I could still feel the heat of where her body had been. It wasn't a memory but something more physical than that: a deep ache in the bones. I wanted to touch her again; I wanted to feel her heat next to mine. I was lost at sea in a darkness full of strange shapes.

The noise of some loud drunks stumbling down the alley woke me up from a restless sleep. Their rowdy insults and loud singing cut through the silence of the night:

"Come on, let's party!
Let's drink some of that good Rey wine,
If not now, then when?"

In the midst of this disturbance—or possibly because of it—an idea flashed across my mind. In one corner of my room there stood a bottle of wine that had been laced with poison so strong it could have killed every sorrow in me with a single sip. But their words, those words that called her a "whore", only made me want her more; they brought her before me glowing and passionate with life in my imaginings. It occurred to me then that I might offer her this fatal draught; we would drink together and die together. What is love to most men? A brief diversion, an ephemeral relationship often couched in vulgar language and expressed in crude terms equally overheard by drunken ears or spoken when sober—like gloating over dirt on one's hand–but for me, it was different.

I must confess: I had known her for years; those mysterious eyes shaped like almonds, lips thin and slightly parted all the time, soft voice...each memory stabbed now at some far-off place in my heart where pain still resided. I wanted back what belonged once upon a time to me but got snatched away instead—I wanted her back.

Was it lost forever? I found this question even scarier. To fight against my unrequited love, I began to enjoy dissatisfaction. I couldn't stop watching the butcher across the street through my window, how he'd roll up his sleeves and say bismillah before slicing through flesh with his blade. This mental image followed me everywhere. Then one day I decided what would make me feel better. So I got out of bed, rolled up my sleeves like his and grabbed for the sharp bone handled knife under my pillow. Pulling on a yellow cape over my shoulders while covering my head and face with a shawl, an uncanny blending occurred between him being there and some old evil thing inside me.

The next day, my wife shouted at me because she found her dress in my bed. We had a fight. But that dress was old and ragged—it was definitely hers—but I wasn't planning on returning it. Why couldn't I keep my wife's dress?

When Nonjoon came in with donkey milk, honey, fresh bread—and a knife with a bone handle on the tray; she said she'd picked it up off the old pig-faced man's carpet and raised her eyebrows saying "good to have a knife to hand,"—I recognized it as mine and took it. "Your wife is pregnant, I saw her bruises at the bathhouse last night." "Maybe the child will take after the old man!" Nonjoon said. Fear shot through me. Nonjoon left looking pale. I put the knife in my chest cloth and closed the door.

The baby could not be mine—it had to belong to the pig-faced man!

That evening, my wife's little brother went into my room. He was the same as her, even down to the nail biting. One look at them would tell you they were blood relatives; same small mouth and full lips; beautifully arched eyelids with almond shaped eyes always puzzled about something; high cheekbones, wild black hair, wheat-colored skin that begged me to taste. It was careless of him too. They both had those irresistible Turkmen eyes that only open onto a troubled life which will never know peace. Life is a struggle for survival and all this living is just to stay alive in this troubled world. These eyes are shaped by their bitter past, filled with the sufferings of survival;

tinged with hopeless hope and inherited pains that will never heal but be passed on.

I knew how his sister's mouth tastes–slightly bitter; laced with opium's shadowed touch. He walked in and looked at me with these bewildered beautiful eyes saying: "Nonjoon says you're a wise man. You will die soon then we can get rid of you. How people usually die?"
"I died long time ago," I replied.

"Whole house would have been ours if our kid hadn't died," he added, quoting Nonjoon.

A laugh so cold and sharp escaped me I scared myself with it; I didn't recognize my own voice. He rushed out of the room in fear.

That is the time I realized why the butcher enjoyed cleaning his knife by scraping its bone handle against the sheep's thigh. He relished cutting through the skin, peeling it back to expose the clotted, mud-like blood underneath. The blood dripped slowly from the sheep's throats to the ground. Beside the butcher's stall, the yellow dog and the fallen sheep heads, with their blank, darkened eyes, watched on. Those sheep heads bore the same expression, as if the dust of death had dimmed their vision.

They knew—the silent witnesses of countless endings, understanding the inevitable cycle they were part of. In the end, I realized I was only half alive, detached from the trivial desires of others. I was enveloped by a sense of eternity, an unending existence. What did forever mean? To me, it was the memory of playing beside the river with that crippled girl, closing my eyes for a moment and resting my head in her lap.

There were times when I caught myself speaking in an unfamiliar tone. I yearned to speak, but my lips felt too heavy to move. Yet, even in their silence, it seemed I was conversing with myself.

The room, which felt increasingly cramped and shadowy like a grave, consumed me in the darkness of the night. I wrapped myself in a cloak and shawl by the dim light of the lamp, and watched my stooped shadow stretch ominously along the wall.

My shadow looked more alive than me, it gave the impression of having taken over my own self. Just like I was surrounded by an old man with a swollen joint, a butcher, Nonjoon and my wife, who were nothing more but the many arms of my shadow that had encircled me. At that moment in time, I felt like an owl even though there were blood rains where my voice was supposed to be heard. Maybe the owl too was sick of thinking along these lines together with me? Glancing at the wall behind me, I saw its shadow taking the shape of an owl that seemed to be reading through what I had written—it understood everything being said—the only real entity there is.

At the sight of my shadow, I was filled with fright. On one dark and still night after another, which seemed to be all my nights, I found myself enclosed by threatening shadows that stared at me from the walls and behind the curtains. Often my room felt so narrow that it seemed like a coffin. My body hurt; it would not move even a bit. There was a weight on my chest that made it hard for me to breathe—just like the one those weak black horses carried when they took meat to the butcher's shop.

Like a mute who tries to repeat each phrase at the end of a verse only to begin again, death's song whispered low. It screamed in my heart like a saw being stopped suddenly by silence after going high and shrill for such a long time.

Right as I closed my eyes, some loud drunk men came past my door yelling and singing:

"Come on, let's party!
Let's drink some of that good Rey wine,

If not now, then when?"

A thought struck me quick: "I might as well go out there and get killed by somebody else!" It filled me with strength; every part of me tingled and cooled down against my skin where it stretched tight over bones. I put on my yellow cloak and let its folds hang from shoulders while covering up most everything else outside world-wise wrapped shawl around head so nobody could see but eyes peering out knife handled bones slid into belt walked towards the most awful haunted room as quiet as shadow moves through space.

As I approached, the door was filled with darkness; thick, dense, impenetrable. I stopped and listened in the silence. A voice came from out of the blackness; it was soft and familiar: "Have you come? Take off your shawl." It sung to me like a lullaby I knew when I was young or like a whisper that reminded me of the wind. It was a voice from my deepest sleep, a voice from long ago. Was this again but another dream? This voice brought back memories of laughter from riverbanks where the little girl used to play; I couldn't move because she called me so powerfully with her words! But then she said them again quieter still—like an invitation—and softer too this time. "Come inside . . . unwrap your shawl."

I stepped slowly into the room, letting fall my cloak and shawl as I went. Even under her coverlet, I kept the knife clutched in my hand; but after a moment her warm sheet started soaking through my skin—its lifeblood gave me back my own vitality. She lay before me slender and white with those enticing Turkmen eyes that had seen so many games on so many rivers in our childhoods together; but I approached her as no predator lunges with hunger or even longing—love and hate were all twisted up together inside me that I could never untangle them again.

She moved her body away from me, like a snake sliding smoothly but still getting everything it wants. Her skin smelled strong; when she put her arms around my neck they were hot. In that moment I wished to die as all anger left me. I saw our legs wrapped together and held back tears while she squeezed more and more tightly. The heat of her tender young flesh gave me another chance while burning my soul drew me nearer to the center of her like a trapper seizes its prey.

There was a mix of fear and joy inside me. Her lips had a salty and bitter taste, adding to her already cucumber-like flavor. But these feelings overshadowed her flaws. I completely surrendered and let her embrace smother me. No other world existed. I told lies to look good. I had no willpower left; everything I wanted was in her, so I never had to worry about disturbing anything. My face was pressed against her jasmine-scented hair, and yet, we were both screaming with the intense happiness we felt all at once.

Struggling to break free felt like wrestling shadows—every effort melted back into a suffocating embrace. In the chaos, my hand flinched, and the cold knife blade slid into soft flesh. Warm blood splattered across my face. Her scream pierced the air, breaking the bond between us as she recoiled from my touch. I tossed the knife away, my hand trembling as I realized the icy stillness of her body against mine.

A coarse laugh erupted from my throat, an unsettling sound that made the fine hairs on my neck stand. Fear gripped me; I draped my cloak over my shoulders and retreated into the shadowed safety of my own room.

By the dim gaslight, I opened my bloodied hand to find her eye resting in my palm. I staggered toward the mirror with shaking hands, trying to avoid the reflection of what I'd become—an old man, ghastly and grotesque. My hair and beard had turned ghostly white, as if I had stumbled out of a lethal encounter. My split and bleeding lip mirrored that of the old man; my eyes, bereft of lashes, stared back at me. A clump of white hair on my chest and a chilling spirit had taken over me. A strange laughter burst from within me, sharp and unsettling. It echoed hollowly through the empty space around me.

I had turned into something repulsive. Dread filled me, like waking from a disturbing dream. I rubbed my eyes, the room dimly lit and windows fogged. In the distance, a rooster crowed, marking a new day, but my brazier held only cold ashes—a silent warning.

My thoughts drooped like wilted funeral flowers. Searching for the ragweed pot the gravedigger had given me, it was gone.

Looking up, I saw a hunched figure against the wall, no longer the robust old man I knew. Wrapped in a shawl, clutching a pot wrapped in a dirty cloth, he laughed—a dry, bone-chilling rasp.

As I tried to confront him, he slipped away, vanishing from my room. I followed, chasing his stooped silhouette down the alley, his shoulders shaking with laughter until he disappeared from view.

Gazing down, I noticed my tattered clothes, my skin adorned with dried blood. Around me, two gold flies buzzed, and tiny white worms wriggled across my flesh. A weight like a corpse pressed down on my chest...